A Peacock on the

written and illustrated by Paul Adshead

"I am proud of this story"
Prince

Published by Child's Play (International) Ltd

© M Twinn 1987
This impression 1989

ISBN 0-85953-295-X (hard cover)
ISBN 0-85953-307-7 (soft cover)

Printed in Singapore

THE PEACOCK FAMILY

If you ask Prince the peacock, he will tell you
this is his story. Prince is vain.

"I am so beautiful and I have such a fine voice.
I should be the ruler of the garden.
So, why does nobody take any notice of me?"

Ask Pavlova the peahen, and she will tell you
that this is her story.

"I have to protect my peachicks, Solomon, Little Prince
and Sweet Pea. That's no easy matter with a cat
like Timothy about. And I get no help from
that good-for-nothing, Prince."

THE CAT

One day, Little Prince was showing off to Solomon.
Sweet Pea sat on Pavlova.

Timothy, stealing softly along a bough, was totally
happy. He is fascinated by anything small with soft,
fluttery feathers.

Nobody knew where Timothy came from. Nobody ever sees
him come and nobody ever sees him go.

Suddenly, Pavlova let out a warning cry.
Little Prince, Solomon and Sweet Pea scurried to safety.

Pavlova launched herself at Timothy. Timothy scampered away.

"The important thing," he thought,
"Is not to win but to play the game."

THE MAN WHO LOVES BIRDS

The Man who loves Birds came out to see
what all the rumpus was about.
Little Prince and Solomon began to follow
his green wellingtons. Not surprising,
since he has cared for the chicks
ever since they left their shells.

But Sweet Pea stayed safely
close to Pavlova, who told her:

"Good girl!
You can't be sure with humans."

When the man returned from the house with food, the chicks began to feed.

"Me first, me first. Feed me first!" complained Prince shrilly. "I am the most important."

But the man said, "Wait your turn, Prince. The chicks have had a scare. Why don't you look out for Timothy, instead of leaving all the work to Pavlova?"

"Enough of your insolence!" screamed Prince, to bring the man to his senses.

And he fanned out his majestic tail feathers.

But the man still did not take any notice.

It was too much for Prince.

"I'm leaving for a better life.
I'm not used to being scolded.
You'll be sorry, yes, you will!"

This time, to his surprise, Prince actually got his feet off the ground, so he kept on flying.

Prince was right. The man was sorry.
Now he had to get out his net and his bicycle
and set out to find Prince.
"Anything might happen to the silly creature,"
he told Toby, the Yorkshire terrier.

In the meantime, Prince had managed another surprising feat,
to land on the roof of a house. Looking back,
his own garden seemed a long way off.

THE CHILDREN

Inside the house lived three children and a handsome tabby cat.
They were all alone and when they saw the man they were frightened.
"He has come to catch us with his big net!" wailed little Bianca.

And the man who preferred birds and dogs and mice,
and even frogs, to cats, did look very strange indeed.

So Anna dialled the police, like she had been shown.
And when the man rang the door bell,
Alex didn't open the door.

But he did lift the letter box flap.

And the man peered through and said,
"Don't be frightened. There's a peacock on the roof,
and I've come to take him home."

But the children didn't believe him and they didn't open the door.

THE POLICEMAN

When Officer Martin arrived, he saw the Man who loves Birds placing a ladder against the wall of the house.

Hmm. Very suspicious.

Officer Martin took out his notebook and his pencil, and began to write.

The Man who loves Birds cleared his throat.

"Good evening, Officer. Let me explain.
There's a peacock on the roof, and I've come to take him home.
It's all perfectly clear, really."

But it wasn't clear. It wasn't clear at all. In fact, it was getting darker all the time. And the peacock was hidden behind the chimney.

THE PARENTS

At this moment the children's parents arrived.
Mrs Williams was cross with Mr Williams.

"Why did I ever listen to you? We should never have left
the children alone," she scolded as they ran towards the house.

When they saw their parents, the children
opened the door. Out bounded the handsome cat,
followed by Anna, Alex and Bianca.

"You did very well to phone the police," Officer Martin told them.
"We'll soon get to the bottom of this."

"But there is a peacock on the roof!" said the Man who loves Birds.

Officer Martin shook his head.

"Now where have I seen that cat before?" thought Toby.
And the next bit of the story is his.

Once he realised that the cat was Timothy,
Toby chased him for all he was worth.
But Timothy ran nimbly up the ladder and onto the roof.

And on the roof Timothy found Prince.

"It's all your fault!" screamed Prince.
"If you hadn't frightened the chicks,
I would have been fed first!"

"It's all your fault!" hissed Timothy.
"And now everybody knows the secret
of where I live."

But Prince didn't stop to argue. With one final screech,
he flapped his wings and set off for home.

"So there was a peacock on the roof!" exclaimed Officer Martin.
And everybody laughed. The nice man said the children
could come to see the garden whenever they wanted.

The children promised they would keep Timothy at home.
"We'll see about that," purred Timothy.

Later that night, two families slept very cosily and safely indeed.

The man who loves Birds dreamed about his friends,
and Prince told Pavlova, ''There's no place like home.''